Fairy Realm

BOOK 3

The Third wish

ALSO BY EMILY RODDA

Fairy Realm

The Third Wish

BOOK 3

EMILY RODDA

ILLUSTRATIONS BY RAOUL VITALE

HARPERCOLLINS*PUBLISHERS*

The Third Wish

Copyright © 2003 by Emily Rodda

www.harperchildrens.com

Library of Congress Cataloging-in-Publication Data
Rodda, Emily.
  The third wish / Emily Rodda. — 1st American ed.
    p.   cm. — (Fairy realm ; book 3)
  Sequel to: The Flower Fairies
  "Originally published under the name Mary-Anne Dickinson as the
Storytelling Charms series, 1994" — CIP data.
  Summary: When her home is threatened by fire, Jessie returns to the
magical world of the Realm and visits the mermaids of the Under-Sea to
search for a wish-stone.
  ISBN 0-06-009589-X — ISBN 0-06-009590-3 (lib. bdg.)
  [1. Wishes—Fiction. 2. Magic—Fiction. 3. Mermaids—Fiction.] I.
Title.
PZ7.R5996 Th 2003   2002027338
[Fic]—dc21   CIP
                                                                     AC

Typography by Karin Paprocki
1   2   3   4   5   6   7   8   9   10
❖
First American Edition
Previously published by ABC Books for the
AUSTRALIAN BROADCASTING CORPORATION
GPO Box 9994 Sydney NSW 2001
Originally published under the name
Mary-Anne Dickinson as the Storytelling Charms Series 1994

CONTENTS

Fairy Realm

book 3

The Third wish

wishes

"I wish I could go to the pool today," sighed Jessie, looking out the Blue Moon kitchen window at the fierce blue sky.

Her mother didn't answer, so Jessie tried again, raising her voice over the sound of the early morning news droning from the radio.

"It's going to be really hot again today," she said. "I *wish* you didn't have to go to work, Mum. Then you could take me swimming."

She looked sideways at her mother. But Rosemary still didn't answer. She didn't even seem to be listening. She switched off the radio and

1

started rushing around with a piece of toast in one hand and her car keys in the other, the belt of her nurses' uniform dangling behind her.

Jessie edged toward her. "I wish it wasn't so *hot*," she complained. "I didn't think it *ever* got as hot as this in the Mountains. I wish we were somewhere cooler. I wish Granny's car was fixed so *she* could take me to the pool. I wish—"

"I wish I could find my sunglasses!" snapped Rosemary. "And I wish you'd stop complaining and being so selfish, Jessie! Think what other people are going through. These terrible fires . . ." She bit her lip and turned away.

Jessie went back to the window and frowned at the sky. There wasn't a cloud to be seen. Just haze from the smoke of burning bushland. And the sun, rising higher, beating down on the house, making everything hot, hot, *hot*.

The clock ticked in the silence of the kitchen.

"At least you don't have to go to school in this heat, Jess," Rosemary said more brightly. "Think yourself lucky you're on holidays."

"Some holiday," grumbled Jessie. "Everyone

else will be at the pool today, while I'll be stuck here, bored and boiling and—"

"Jessie, that's *enough*!" Rosemary exploded.

Jessie jumped, then stuck out her bottom lip and sulked. Her mother hardly ever shouted at her, and she didn't like it.

Granny came into the room with her big ginger cat, Flynn, at her heels. She was frowning, and her green eyes looked worried.

"I met Hazel Bright on my walk," she said. "She says that another big fire broke out early this morning—just outside Silvervale."

"So I just heard on the news," Rosemary answered, as she struggled to fasten her belt. "They're fighting it with everything they've got. But people are starting to panic. It's panic that's the real killer, you know. People forget to think when they panic."

She shook her head. "It's going to be a bad day. It's so dry, Mum. Everything's so dry. And this heat—and the wind . . ."

"Dreadful," nodded Granny. "If only it would rain." She sighed. Flynn twined around her legs.

Rosemary shrugged. "If only," she said. "But wishing won't make it happen, will it?"

She found her sunglasses behind the teapot, put them on, and hurriedly ate the last of her toast. "Well, I'm late," she said. "I'll have to go." She looked seriously at Granny. "Now, Mum, ring me if you're worried about anything, won't you?" she murmured. "I don't like leaving you and Jessie here without the car."

"Don't worry, dear," Granny said. "I know what to do. All will be well."

"I hope so." Rosemary picked up her handbag. "You be good for Granny, now, Jessie," she warned. "Do everything she says. And no more carrying on about the pool. Go and paddle in the fish pond or something."

"*Yes*, Mum," said Jessie. She hunched her shoulders and turned away to look out the window again. "I wish *I* was a fish," she muttered.

She heard her mother click her tongue crossly, but didn't look around.

Granny didn't say anything until Rosemary had gone. Then she walked over to Jessie, her eyes twinkling, and tickled the back of her neck. The charm bracelet on her wrist jingled like tiny bells.

"Don't be crabby, Jessie," she teased.

"Mum's the crabby one," said Jessie shortly. "She's been crabby for days."

"She's hot, she's tired and she's worried about the fires," Granny said. "At the hospital they're treating lots of people who've been injured trying to save their homes. It must be very hard for Rosemary—for all the doctors and nurses. Most of them are probably worried about their own houses and families too."

"Mum doesn't have to worry about *that*, though, does she?" Jessie demanded. "So . . ."

She broke off as she caught sight of Granny's grave face.

"She's *not* worried about it, is she?" she squeaked. "I mean, there's no danger *Blue Moon* could get burned, is there?"

Flynn meowed loudly. Granny bent to stroke his head. "Nothing's safe in this part of the Mountains at the moment, Jessie," she said gently.

"Not even Blue Moon."

Jessie stared at her, open-mouthed. She could hardly take it in. It seemed impossible that the old home she loved so much could be in danger.

"The fires are moving closer to us all the time," Granny went on. "Didn't you hear what we said about Silvervale? That's not far from here at all. And they're fighting to save houses there right now."

Jessie's heart thudded. "I didn't think," she whispered. "I didn't know. Why didn't Mum tell me before?"

"Rosemary didn't want you to be frightened," said Granny calmly. "But I think it's time you understood how things are. You and I both know that you can be very brave if you try. The charms on your bracelet are proof of that."

Jessie glanced at the charm bracelet on her wrist, took a deep breath, and nodded.

Her life had changed in more ways than one since she and Rosemary had come to live with Granny at Blue Moon. Because right at the beginning Jessie had discovered her grandmother's secret—the invisible Door at the bottom of the garden that led to the fairy world where Granny had been born. The world called the Realm.

In the Realm Jessie had had some amazing adventures. And at the end of each of them she'd been given a charm by the Realm Folk, so she'd never forget.

Forget? she thought now, looking at the charms one by one. As if she could ever forget the Realm, or the wonderful, exciting times she had had there. But, she remembered, there had been some hard and dangerous times too. Often she'd had to be brave. Braver than she'd ever thought she could be.

Even so, the idea that her beloved Blue Moon might burn down was very frightening indeed.

It must be frightening to her mother too, she realized. Now she understood why Rosemary, usually so calm and cheerful, had been scratchy and impatient over the last couple of days. And imagine how Granny must feel!

She looked at her grandmother, whose eyes were thoughtful as she scratched Flynn's upturned chin. Blue Moon had been her home ever since she had left the Realm as a young princess, to marry the human man she loved.

Jessie clasped her hands tightly. "Granny," she said. "Can't *you* do something about the fires?"

"If that were possible, I'd have done it long ago, Jessie," Granny said. "I still have some powers, that's true. But it takes very, very powerful magic to change the weather."

"Could Queen Helena do it, then?" Jessie asked. "I could go and ask her." She jumped up, filled with excitement. "Yes! Queen Helena is your sister. She'd want to help. I could . . ."

But Granny was shaking her head. "Helena can't help us either, Jessie," she said. "In the mortal world her magic is no stronger than mine."

But Jessie wasn't going to give up so easily. "Well, isn't there anyone else?" she cried. "Surely there must be *someone* in the Realm whose magic will work here strongly enough. Someone—or something . . ."

She broke off. Granny's face had grown suddenly thoughtful.

"What is it?" Jessie exclaimed, clapping her hands.

Granny touched her charm bracelet with long, slim fingers. "Something," she murmured. "Yes, of course. How could I have forgotten?" She frowned. "It's been so long since I've even thought about them, you see."

"What?" Jessie begged.

"Well," Granny said slowly, "when you said 'something,' I suddenly remembered. About wish-stones."

CHAPTER TWO

A warning

"What are wish-stones?" Jessie asked eagerly. "Do they make wishes come true? What do they look like?"

"Come with me," Granny said. She walked briskly from the kitchen, and Jessie followed.

Granny led the way to the studio where her husband Robert, Jessie's grandfather, had painted the fantasy pictures that had made him famous.

Everyone thought that Robert Belairs had just imagined those scenes of fairy Folk, gnomes, elves, mermaids and miniature horses he painted so beautifully. Jessie used to think so too. But now she knew better.

Grandpa had painted things he had actually seen, in the Realm. Long ago, he, like Jessie, had discovered the Door to the fairy world. And, like her, he had visited it often.

The visits had stopped, of course, the day he and Granny had run away to get married. He couldn't go back after that. Granny's parents had been angry with him, and with their daughter. A fairy princess marrying a human man? Giving up her right to rule as true Queen? That was unheard of in the Realm.

But Granny had never been sorry about the choice she had made. In time her parents had forgiven her. And she was very happy at Blue Moon. Though she was now the Realm's true Queen, her kind sister Helena ruled in her place. And Granny lived on in the mortal world that was now her home.

Robert Belairs was dead now, but his paintings of the Realm had been printed in books and hung in art galleries all over the world. Many of them were on the walls at Blue Moon too. Jessie loved them.

Every painting seemed to sparkle with magic.

Jessie looked around the studio. It still smelled and looked the same as it had when Grandpa was alive. Everything was just as he'd left it.

Granny crossed the room to a small desk in one corner. She picked something up and held it out for Jessie to see.

"There you are, Jessie," she said. "A wish-stone."

"But that's just the stone Grandpa used to hold down his papers," Jessie cried in disappointment.

She'd seen it often, when she'd come to the studio to watch Grandpa paint. She'd held it in her hand and played with it, many times. It was that kind of stone. Smooth, rounded and a speckly-gray color, it fitted into your hand as though it liked to be there. But there was nothing magic about it. Nothing at all.

Granny stroked the stone. "Robert kept it because it reminded him of the Realm," she said. "But it's empty. The wishes are gone."

"Gone?" Jessie didn't understand.

"Every wish-stone can grant three wishes,"

Granny explained. "Once the wishes have been used up, the stone is—just a stone. It looks the same, but it has no magic power any more. Like a battery that's dead."

"But how can you tell?" Jessie asked. "I mean, are you *sure* this one is empty?"

Granny nodded. "Oh yes. You can tell by the way it feels. Anyone from the Realm can tell a live wish-stone from an empty one. Live ones make your fingers tingle."

Jessie licked her lips nervously. "Would *I* be able to tell?" she said.

"Probably," said Granny cheerfully. "After all, you *are* my granddaughter." Then, as Jessie's eyes lit up, she shook her head.

"But we can't depend on a wish-stone to stop the fires, Jessie," she said. "You can't just go to the Realm and find one, if that's what you're thinking." She put the wish-stone back on Robert's desk and walked to the studio door.

"Why not?" asked Jessie, running after her.

"Because wish-stones are very rare," Granny answered. She began leading Jessie down the hall and back to the kitchen. "They're found in Under-Sea, the mermaids' domain. Realm Folk only find them when they are washed up on the shore of the Bay. Realm Folk don't visit Under-Sea."

"Grandpa did," Jessie said, pointing at one of her favorite paintings. It had hung on the wall at the end of the Blue Moon hallway for as long as she could remember.

The painting showed mermaids and mermen swimming in a garden of light green seaweed and palest pink coral. Brightly colored fish flitted through the coral like birds. Tiny, fairy-like creatures with pretty silver fins instead of wings rode seahorses over soft white sand.

In the center of the picture two handsome merpeople sat on a smooth rock, playing with a small mermaid child with light brown hair. A young mermaid with shining black hair stood nearby. Behind them, the crystal spires of palaces shone through transparent blue water.

Granny turned to look at the painting. "Yes," she agreed. "Robert often went to Under-Sea. Being human, he was always welcome in the merpeople's palaces. Realm Folk are not. It is the Rule."

"Granny, I'm a human," Jessie exclaimed. "Or mostly. So I can go to Under-Sea and bring back a wish-stone!"

Granny stared at her. "I suppose you could try," she began slowly. "But . . ." She hesitated.

Jessie jumped up and down impatiently. "What, Granny?"

"If you *do* find a wish-stone, you must be very, very careful, Jessie. Wish-stones can be very dangerous."

"How?"

"They are very powerful," Granny said. "In all the Realm there is only one wish-granter more powerful. Whoever holds a wish-stone can wish for almost anything, and that wish will come true. But the wish is forever. You can't take it back."

"But that's wonderful, isn't it?" Jessie couldn't see the problem.

"It's wonderful," Granny agreed. "But surely you can see that it's very dangerous too, Jessie? Just think of all the wishes you've made this morning."

Jessie shook her head in bewilderment. The wishes she'd made this morning? What was wrong with them?

"Think about it," Granny urged.

Jessie thought. She'd wished she could go to the pool. She'd wished her mother didn't have to go to work. She'd wished Granny's car was fixed. She'd wished it wasn't so hot.

But then, with Granny's eyes looking gravely into her own, Jessie remembered another wish she'd made. She'd wished she was a fish.

She thought about what might have happened if she'd been holding a wish-stone in her hand when she made that wish, and she felt sick.

Granny nodded. She could see from Jessie's face that she'd finally understood.

"So you see, Jessie," she said gravely, "sometimes we all make wishes that we don't really mean. And of course that doesn't matter at all, usually. But with a wish-stone it does matter. It matters a lot."

"Yes, I see." Jessie swallowed. "I'll be careful, Granny," she promised. "I really will. If I find a wish-stone I won't make any silly wishes. I won't even *think* them."

"Well, see that you don't." Granny tried smile. "How would I explain it to Rosemary if she came home to find you had fins and a tail?"

She patted Jessie's shoulder. "All right," she said. "If you're going, you'd better get ready as quickly as you can. There's no time to lose."

CHAPTER THREE

TO the palace

J essie and Granny walked down from the house, through the trees, to the tall hedge that surrounded the place they called the secret garden. The grass was crisp and dry under their feet, and a scorching wind tossed the branches above them.

Jessie was wearing only a light sundress, with her swimsuit underneath, but she felt very hot all the same. Hot—and frightened.

She followed Granny through the opening in the hedge and stood with her on the smooth grass in the center of the secret garden. She breathed in the tangy scent of rosemary rising from

21

the bushes clustered around the edge of the lawn.

Usually Jessie felt peaceful as soon as she entered the secret garden. It was as though the tall hedge kept the whole world out. But today the smell of smoke mingled with the scent of rosemary. Today the air was filled with fear.

"Now," Granny said. "The first thing you must do is go to the palace. You'll need help to get to the Bay."

Jessie nodded. Her friend, Patrice, was the housekeeper at the palace. Patrice was always glad to see her. And perhaps Maybelle, the bossy miniature horse, and Giff the elf would be there too. They would help her. She knew they would.

"Be back by afternoon-tea time," Granny warned. "No later." She looked up at the hazy sky. "The fires are getting closer," she murmured.

She spun round to face Jessie. "All right," she said. "Go! Go quickly!"

She held up her hand. "Open!" she commanded.

Jessie heard the familiar rushing sound as the Door began to open. She closed her eyes and felt the cool breeze surround her, lifting her long red hair off her shoulders and blowing it around her head.

Then suddenly she remembered something.

"Granny," she called. "If the wish-stones are the second most powerful wish-granters in the Realm, what's the first?"

With the sound of the opening Door filling her ears and her mind, she struggled to hear Granny's answer. It could be important. If she couldn't find a wish-stone, maybe she could dare to go to the most powerful wish-granter of all to get the fires stopped.

But when Granny's answer came, sounding small and far away, she was very surprised.

"Magic fish," Granny called.

Fish? Had Granny really said "fish"?

Jessie strained her ears to hear over the rising and falling of the wind. "Magic fish," cried Granny's voice. "But don't . . . magic fish . . . rules . . . Under-Sea . . . no use . . ."

Then her voice disappeared completely, and Jessie was whirling away.

Into the Realm.

❈   ❈   ❈

Jessie opened her eyes and blinked in the golden light. She had arrived.

The pebbly road was solid under her feet. Behind her, the magic hedge that protected the Realm from invaders stood green and glossy.

Everything looked beautiful and peaceful as always. The sky was a soft, clear blue. The trees by the roadway whispered gently to each other.

And there, nibbling grass under the shade of one of the trees, was a tiny white horse.

"Maybelle!" Jessie called out in delight.

The little horse lifted her head. The red ribbons in her mane fluttered in the breeze. Jessie ran to hug her.

"Well, well, well!" exclaimed Maybelle. "Where did you spring from?"

"I've come because I need help," Jessie said. "I need to find a wish-stone."

Maybelle snorted. "Oh, is that all? No problem!"

Jessie's mouth fell open. "No problem?"

"Oh no!" Maybelle pawed the ground. "Anything else you'd like, while we're at it? The ten crowns of Lillalong? The golden horn of the unicorn? The giant pearl of silence? A sensible brain for Giff the elf?"

Jessie smiled to hide her disappointment. "Oh, you're teasing me," she said.

"Just a bit," said Maybelle. She tossed her mane and showed her teeth in a horse laugh. Then, catching sight of Jessie's face, she stopped laughing.

"Something's wrong," she said.

"Yes," sighed Jessie. "Maybelle, I really, *really* need to find a wish-stone. Blue Moon's in danger. And not only Blue Moon. There are terrible bushfires in the Mountains. The fire-fighters can't stop them. We need rain. We need it now! You've got to help me!"

Maybelle frowned. "I'll do what I can. But finding wish-stones isn't easy, you know," she warned.

"I know," said Jessie. "Granny told me. But I'm going to Under-Sea to try."

Maybelle snorted with shock. "Under-Sea?" she repeated. "Queen Jessica said you could go *there*?" She paused. "Listen, I think you'd better go and see Patrice about this," she said. "She'll know what's best to do."

She trotted off toward the road with Jessie following.

"What if Patrice isn't home?" Jessie worried, as they began walking toward the palace.

"Oh, she is," said Maybelle. "Or she *was*, half an hour ago. I was there myself, but I had to leave. Giff was with her. I had to get away from him before he drove me crazy. He's being sillier than usual today, and that's saying something."

Jessie giggled. She couldn't help it. She might be excited, and worried, and even a little bit scared. But the thought of Giff always made her laugh.

The great front doors of Queen Helena's golden palace were standing wide open, but Maybelle and Jessie slipped around to the little side door that led to Patrice's own apartment.

Jessie knocked.

In a moment she heard footsteps, and then the door was opened.

"Jessie!" cried Patrice. She held out her arms,

and her black button eyes shone. "How lovely to see you! Giff's just gone to the palace kitchen on an errand for me, but he'll be back soon."

"Worse luck," growled Maybelle, nudging Jessie forward with her nose. "Now listen, Patrice. You and I have a big problem to solve. Jessie wants us to help her find—wait for it—a wish-stone!"

She nodded solemnly at Patrice, who was staring at Jessie in surprise.

"That's right," Maybelle went on. "A wish-stone. Jessie needs it. Badly. I've told her wish-stones are impossible to find. But she—"

"I don't know about impossible," Patrice called back over her shoulder, as she led them down the narrow corridor to her kitchen.

"Is that right?" snorted Maybelle. "I suppose you can tell us just where one is, then, can you?"

They went into Patrice's cozy kitchen, and Jessie sat down at the table in her usual place.

Patrice bustled to the cupboard. "As a matter of fact, Maybelle," she said, pulling down a cookie tin from the top shelf, "I can."

Maybelle sniffed. "Go on, then," she jeered. "If you're so smart!"

Patrice smiled. And from the cookie tin she pulled a round, gray-speckled wish-stone!

CHAPTER FOUR

giff gets into trouble

Jessie sprang to her feet. Her chair crashed to the floor behind her. "Patrice!" she yelled. "You've got one! You've got a wish-stone!"

Maybelle shook her head at the stone lying on the table. She nuzzled it with her nose and jumped back. "It's a live one too."

"Of course it is," said Patrice.

"But where did you get it?" demanded Maybelle.

Patrice shrugged her plump shoulders. She looked a bit embarrassed. "I took a splinter out of a griffin's wing a couple of weeks ago, and the next day it brought me the stone. It must have had it

31

for years and years."

"Humph!" Maybelle pawed the floor. "Pretty good thank-you present."

"Yes," Patrice admitted. "I tried to give it back but the griffin wouldn't take it. You know how they are. It's not full, you know. By the feel of it, it's only got one wish left in it. Anyway, I was saving that for a special occasion. And it looks as if this is it."

"You mean I can *have* this stone?" cried Jessie. She couldn't believe her luck.

"Of course you can, dearie," said Patrice warmly. "After all you've done for the Realm, it's the least I can do. Now, sit down again and tell me what's been going on." She put a jug of cool-looking pink drink on the table, and went back to the cupboard to get out another cookie jar.

"Well, this *is* handy," said Maybelle, watching Jessie rescue her fallen chair and draw it up to the table. "Now you won't have to go to Under-Sea, Jessie. And a good thing too."

Patrice, coming back with a plate of honey

snaps, looked shocked. "I should think so!" she exclaimed.

"But why shouldn't I have gone?" Jessie asked. Of course she was very happy to have found a wish-stone so quickly and easily, but in her heart she was rather sorry that now she didn't have an excuse to visit the mermaids.

"It's *much* too dangerous." Patrice shook her head. "*Much*!"

"Granny didn't think so," protested Jessie.

Patrice looked puzzled. "How *could* Queen Jessica be happy for Jessie to go to Under-Sea? With Lorca sitting in the Bay on that horrible Island, just waiting to—"

"Who—" Jessie began.

"I know why," Maybelle broke in. "It's because Lorca and the Island only appeared about fifty years ago. You remember, Patrice. At the blue moon. The time of the renewal of the magic."

"Oh, of *course*," sighed Patrice. "And Jessica left the Realm at around the same time, with Robert. So she never heard about Lorca. She thinks Under-Sea is still as safe as it used to be."

"Who's Lorca?" asked Jessie, getting her question in at last.

Patrice shuddered. "Better not to know, dearie," she said. "You won't have to worry about her now, anyway. You've got your stone. You've got your wish. Have a cookie."

"Cookie?" squeaked a voice from the door.

"Here's trouble," growled Maybelle.

Giff the elf came tiptoeing into the room. He squealed when he saw Jessie, and ran to sit down beside her, his big pointed ears waggling with excitement.

Jessie was delighted to see him.

Maybelle was not so pleased. "For goodness' sake, sit still, Giff," she humphed. "Don't talk, don't wriggle, don't do anything."

"Can I have a cookie?" Giff asked in a small voice.

Patrice laughed as she poured the drinks. "I suppose so," she said. "But just one. You've already had three this morning."

Giff helped himself, beaming. He wriggled closer to Jessie. "Honey snaps are my favorite," he whispered to her.

He swallowed the last crumb and his eyes darted back to the plate. His fingers crept across the table.

Maybelle made a disgusted sound, then bent to drink.

"No more honey snaps, Giff," warned Patrice, turning away to refill the jug.

"I wasn't!" protested Giff, looking guilty. His fingers swerved from the cookie plate to the stone lying beside it. "I was just looking at this."

He picked up the stone. "But it's not fair," he whimpered, playing with it while he looked longingly at the plate. "I *adore* honey snaps."

"Ah, Giff," murmured Jessie. "I don't think you'd better—"

Maybelle's head jerked up sharply.

"I could eat a million of them," sighed Giff.

"Giff!" shouted Maybelle. "Put that—"

"I wish I *had* a million of them, all to myself, right now."

There was a cracking sound and a puff of smoke.

Giff screamed. And then Jessie was screaming too. Because suddenly she couldn't move. She couldn't see. She was buried in a mountain. A mountain made of a million honey snap cookies.

It took a long time for them to get out of Patrice's kitchen. The honey snaps were piled as high as the ceiling and had blocked the door. But finally, mainly thanks to Maybelle's strong hoofs, they were all standing out in the air, brushing themselves down.

"What's happened?" Giff wailed. "Why do these things always happen to me?"

"Because you're a meddling, idiotic elf who can't keep his hands to himself, that's why!" roared Maybelle, stamping her feet. Cookie crumbs sprayed from her mane in a honey-smelling shower.

Patrice was furious too. "That was a *wish-stone*

36

you were playing with, Giff. A *wish-stone!*" she raged. "And now you've used up the last wish. You . . . you . . ."

"I didn't know!" squealed poor Giff. "I didn't know! It's not my fault!"

"Whose fault is it then?" hissed Maybelle. "Jessie *needed* that wish. She needed it badly. And now it's gone."

Giff began to sob as though his heart was broken. His ears drooped miserably.

Jessie put her arms around him. "Giff, it's all right," she said. "I know it was an accident. Don't cry." She bit her lip. She was terribly upset and disappointed. But she couldn't bear to see Giff so sad.

"I'll just go to Under-Sea, as I'd planned," she went on. "I'll find another wish-stone."

Giff sobbed even more loudly. "To Under-Sea?" he wept. "But, Jessie, if you go there Lorca might get you, like she got that young mermaid, long ago. And all those other creatures since. Oh no! And it will be all my fault!"

"Jessie," Patrice exclaimed. "You absolutely can *not* go to —"

"I have to go!" Jessie insisted. "There's no way out of it now."

Giff groaned and buried his face in his hands.

Maybelle was slowly shaking her head.

"Please, Maybelle," Jessie begged. "Please. You've got to show me the way to Under-Sea."

Maybelle shut her eyes and went on shaking her head. "No, no, no!"

Jessie stuck out her chin stubbornly. "Well, if you won't show me the way, Maybelle, I'll just find someone else who will!" she said.

Maybelle opened her eyes and looked deep into Jessie's own. Then she sighed. "All right," she said. "If you're determined to do this, I suppose I can't stop you. I'll take you as far as the Bay. But after that you'll be on your own, Jessie. I can't go with you to Under-Sea. None of us can."

Jessie's stomach gave a nasty little lurch. But she knew she had no choice. If Blue Moon was going to be saved, she had to find a wish-stone.

And if Under-Sea was where wish-stones were found, Under-Sea was where she had to try, whatever the danger.

Maybelle tossed her head. "Well, if we're going, let's go." She began trotting down the pathway beside the palace.

Giff's lips trembled. He clutched at Jessie's skirt. "I'm coming too," he said.

"Well, I'm staying," said Patrice grimly. "To clean a million honey snaps out of my kitchen. Though how I'll ever do it I don't know."

She thought for a moment, then she nodded. "I'll get the Palace Guards to come and help me with it," she said. "They all love honey snaps. They'll eat the kitchen clean in no time."

"Good!" said Jessie. She hugged the little housekeeper goodbye. "Now, don't worry about me, Patrice," she said. "And thank you for offering me your wish."

"Take great care, Jessie," Patrice whispered. "Come back to us safely."

With a final wave, Jessie and Giff scuttled after

Maybelle, down the narrow path.

"Where does this lead?" Jessie asked.

"To the river," wailed Giff. "To the wet, cold, scary, watery, awful river!"

CHAPTER FIVE

The River

Giff was still sniffling when they reached the river. Jessie sighed. She wished he wouldn't. Crying wasn't going to help. And besides, though she was feeling scared at the thought of the adventure ahead of her, she couldn't help feeling rather excited too.

The river was beautiful. Through its sparkling pale blue water, where tiny silver fish darted, you could see a bed of smooth white pebbles. Grass and flowers grew thickly along its banks, and it wound away into the distance like a ribbon laid out on a green carpet.

Maybelle trotted to the water's edge and stood there peering back toward a bend in the stream.

"What's Maybelle looking for?" Jessie asked Giff, hoping to take his mind off his troubles.

"A river-float," sniffed Giff. He blew his nose on a large green-and-white-spotted handkerchief. "One should be coming along any time now. Just be ready to jump in when it arrives. Those awful flying fish don't like to wait. They're *so* impatient."

Flying fish?

Jessie was just about to ask some more questions when she heard a strange sound. A whistling, splashing sound.

"At last!" snorted Maybelle.

Jessie looked up, and caught her first glimpse of a Realm river-float. It rounded the river bend and came speeding toward them, dazzling in the sun. Whatever she'd been expecting, it was nothing like this!

Six great silver fish, with rainbow fins spread wide, leaped together like dolphins through the pale blue water. Behind them, pulled by silver ribbons and skimming on a froth of white bubbles, raced a curved float that gleamed like glass.

The whistling sound grew louder. The river water began lapping up onto the grass. Jessie's heart thudded with excitement.

"Hold up your hands!" ordered Maybelle. "Get ready!"

The flying fish saw the waving hands and steered for shore. While their passengers piled into the rocking float, they tossed their heads impatiently. Water sprayed from their rainbow fins and scattered in sparkling drops from the silver ribbons.

"Hold on tight," Maybelle warned the others. She settled herself in the front of the float, behind the fish. "Ready?"

At the back of the float, Giff whimpered and clung to Jessie. The craft heaved and dipped in the water. Jessie held tightly to the smooth, glassy edge and grabbed Giff's coat with her free hand. She didn't want him to fall overboard.

The fish made a clicking noise and swished their tails. Jessie could tell that they were anxious to be on their way.

"To the Bay!" called Maybelle, nudging at the silver ribbons. And with a mighty leap the fish were off, the float speeding behind them.

Within moments they had reached full speed and had begun to sing their strange, whistling song again. And then the float started to skim over the surface of the water like a hovercraft. It was almost flying on a carpet of bubbles. Jessie gasped with delight as the wind beat into her face.

"Isn't this *wonderful!*" she squealed to Giff beside her.

Giff moaned softly. His eyes were tightly closed and he was looking very pale. Jessie hoped he wouldn't be sick.

They flew along, leaving a trail of white froth behind them. On each side the green banks slipped away. Every now and then Jessie saw a village surrounded by fields of pink flowers and golden grass, or a group of miniature horses grazing, or elf children hanging from the trees, waving and calling. Sometimes there were green-haired water sprites too, staring silently at them from their secret homes behind the reeds that grew at the river's edge.

Jessie lost all track of time. She stared till her eyes were sore as the countryside flashed by. She didn't want to miss anything.

"Won't be long now," called Maybelle. "The Bay is up ahead."

Over the backs of the flashing, leaping fish, Jessie saw the broad blue waters of the Bay, ringed with rocks and white sand. She shook her head in amazement. How could they have reached it so quickly? It seemed to her that they had been traveling for only a few minutes. Had they been going so fast?

Maybelle saw her surprise. "Time goes fast on the river, Jessie," she shouted over the whistling of the flying fish.

"Not fast enough for me," whispered Giff.

The float began to slow down. The fish swerved toward the bank.

"This is as far as they go," called Maybelle. "From here we walk down to the Bay. Then I'll call an Under-Sea guide for you."

Before Jessie could ask her what she meant,

the float had swept around on its ribbons and bumped gently into the bank. The fish began making their clicking noises and thrashing their tails.

"Out!" ordered Maybelle.

Jessie and Giff scrambled out onto a neat square of sand covered with white pebbles like the ones on the riverbed. Jessie stumbled and almost fell. Her knees felt wobbly and her head swam.

She realized that whatever she had thought, they really must have been on the river for quite a long time. It had been early morning when they started off, but now the sun was much higher in the perfect blue sky. No wonder her legs felt strange, walking on dry land after hours cramped up on the speeding float.

She sniffed the salty, sea-smelling air and blinked at the countryside around her: low bushes studded with small purple flowers, blue-green grass poking through sandy ground.

Maybelle clambered from the float, the ribbons in her mane fluttering in the breeze. She turned and dipped her head to the silver fish.

"Thank you," she called.

The fish raised and lowered their rainbow fins in reply. And then they leaped away from the bank, turned, and sped back the way they had come, the empty float skimming behind them. Their whistling song floated back to Jessie as they disappeared into the distance, leaving a trail of white behind them. Soon they were out of sight, and only the splashing of the water on the riverbank showed where they had passed.

Following Maybelle, and holding Giff by the hand, Jessie climbed up from the riverbank to a low hill and looked out over the Bay.

It was calm and still. Water rippled gently against the white sand of the beach. Beyond the Bay Jessie could see the deeper blue of the open sea, stretching away into the distance. But guarding the entrance to the sea, right in the middle of the gap, was the dark, jagged shape of a rocky island. It looked like a blot on a pretty picture — out of place and ugly.

Jessie felt Giff's hand tighten on hers and she shivered. She felt very far away from home now. Very far away from the palace and the Door that led to the secret garden at Blue Moon. She thought of the fires. Of Granny waiting for her and trusting her. Would she be able to find a wish-stone before it was too late?

"Once upon a time you could have found a wish-stone anywhere along there, if you looked long and hard enough," Maybelle said, nodding at the white shore of the Bay. "They used to get washed up on the sand once in a while. But now . . ."

"What happened?" Jessie asked.

"Some Folk say that when Lorca's Island came up out of the sea, it changed the way the tide worked," Giff said. "They say that's why the wish-stones aren't washed up here any more."

"The Island came up out of the sea?" exclaimed Jessie. "Just like that?"

Maybelle nodded, frowning at the ugly Island. "Lorca's magic must be very powerful," she said. "One day the Bay was clear. The next, the Island was sitting there, right at the entrance. Blocking the way to the open sea."

"You could swim around it," Jessie pointed out. "Or sail."

"You could," Maybelle agreed. "And the fish and mermaids and other creatures do move in and out, of course. They have to, to gather food. But they keep well away from the Island. If creatures swim too close, or the tide sweeps them too near its shores, they are drawn into it. And no one ever sees them again."

Jessie stared at her in horror. "But how awful!" she cried. "Why doesn't Queen Helena stop it?"

Maybelle flicked her mane. "Queen Helena does not interfere with the workings of Under-Sea," she said. "The creatures of Under-Sea love her as their Queen, but rule their own domain. That is the Rule."

Jessie shook her head. "Who is this Lorca? Where did she come from?"

"No one knows," said Giff. "She just . . . appeared one day, at the time of the blue moon."

"We didn't take much notice at first," Maybelle added. "Just then no one cared much about anything except the news that Princess Jessica had left the Realm. But then we heard that a young mermaid had been taken. And now everyone fears the

Island. You must keep well away from it, Jessie."

Jessie nodded. "Of *course*, Maybelle," she said. The idea of going anywhere near that black rock in the Bay scared her to death. She wasn't going to fall into the evil Lorca's clutches. No way.

CHAPTER SIX

Ripple

Maybelle made her way down the narrow, overgrown path that led to the Bay. Jessie followed. The purple-flowered bushes tickled her bare legs as she walked, and the sand was warm under her feet. She could hear Giff stumbling along behind her.

Soon the three friends were standing on the soft white sand. Strange shells and pieces of seaweed lay in heaps along the shore. Crystal-clear water lapped gently at their feet. Giff squeaked and jumped back as it reached for his toes.

Near to where they were standing was a huge

bell, like an old-fashioned school bell, hanging low to the ground. It looked as though it hadn't been used for a very long time. Salt crusted its golden surface, and grass had grown up around the short wooden posts on which it hung. Maybelle plodded over to it.

"All right, then," she said, shaking her mane. "Are you ready?"

Suddenly Jessie didn't feel ready for anything. "What do I do?" she whispered.

"You don't do anything," said Maybelle. "You just stand and wait."

She turned her back on the bell and kicked out with her back legs, striking it with her tiny hoofs once, twice, three times.

A low ringing sound filled Jessie's head. She put her hands over her ears, but still she could feel the ringing through her fingers. She saw the waters of the Bay start to shimmer. Small caps of foam appeared here and there.

"Oh, stop it, stop it!" squealed Giff, wrapping his arms around his head.

Maybelle bared her teeth. The sound was

hurting her ears too, but she scanned the water in silence, watching carefully for any sign that her message had been heard.

Slowly the ringing died away. Jessie took her hands from her ears.

"Nothing's happening at all," she exclaimed in disappointment.

"Wait," murmured Maybelle. "Stand still and wait."

Jessie did as she was told. The small waves rippled over her toes. The warm sun beat on her back and shoulders.

"There," said Maybelle at last. "There!"

Jessie squinted at the shining water. At first she couldn't see anything. And then she drew a sharp breath of excitement. A groove in the surface was moving swiftly toward them. It was as if something was swimming deep down, very fast.

She rubbed at her eyes and stared again at the water. A shape was rising slowly up out of the depths.

The shape came closer and closer. And then, suddenly, a head crowned with a mass of floating light-brown hair broke through the surface. A sweet, pale face was smiling at her. And then there were white shoulders and arms, and the glistening silver of a tail.

A mermaid!

Jessie swallowed. She didn't know what to do or say.

Maybelle stepped forward and nudged at her, pushing her further into the water.

"This human child wishes entrance to Under-Sea," she said. "Will you guide her?"

The mermaid bowed her head. She lifted her hands from the water and threw something. Jessie caught it. It was a necklace, made of shells and pink coral.

"Put it on," said Maybelle.

"Do I have to?" whispered Jessie. The necklace looked pretty but it was hard and prickly, and she was sure it would be uncomfortable to wear.

"Yes," Maybelle told her. "You'll need it. Unless you can breathe better under the water than most humans can. And be quick, Jessie. She won't wait for you long."

Jessie understood. She pulled off her sundress so that she was just wearing her swimsuit. She threw the dress onto the sand. Then she slipped the necklace over her head. The mermaid watched her with large, unblinking blue eyes.

Maybelle shook her head. "I don't like this," she said. "I wish I could go with you."

"I'll be all right, Maybelle," Jessie answered firmly. But she sounded much braver than she felt. Only the thought of Blue Moon made her step forward. She started wading out into the water, toward the mermaid. The water reached her waist . . . her chest . . . her shoulders . . .

"We'll wait for you, Jessie," Giff called. "However long it takes, we'll be here."

Jessie turned back to see that he had picked up her dress and was clutching it in his arms. He was trying to be brave, but tears were rolling down his cheeks. Maybelle was looking straight ahead, her eyes dark with fear, her mane whipping in the wind.

Jessie stood on tiptoe and lifted her arm to wave. Cool fingers, soft as velvet, grasped her other hand. She looked around. The mermaid was beside her, smiling. A smooth tail brushed against her legs.

› And then the fingers were pulling her out of her depth, and the water was closing over her head. And she was being drawn down, down, away from the land and the air and the sunlight. Into Under-Sea.

Jessie was seized with panic. Everything had happened too quickly.

She struggled desperately against the mermaid's grip, but the cool fingers, so soft to touch, were strong. She couldn't get away. Her eyes were shut tight, her head was spinning. She felt as though her lungs were bursting.

"Breathe, little human, breathe, or you will die." The voice rippled and sighed in her head. It was like nothing she had ever heard before. She forced her eyes to open.

The mermaid was facing her, her own beautiful blue eyes wide. Her tail moved gently in the water.

Her hair floated around her face and shoulders like a cloud.

"Breathe!" There was the voice again. But the mermaid hadn't moved her lips.

Then Jessie realized that the sound was in her mind. The mermaid was speaking to her without using her voice. She was so surprised that she gasped. Bubbles of air escaped from her mouth and lungs.

"Breathe!" insisted the gentle voice.

Jessie did. She knew she had no choice. And the moment she began, she knew that the magic of the necklace had worked. She could breathe just as easily in this clear salty water as she could on land.

She almost laughed with relief.

The mermaid smiled and let go of her hand. "My name is Ripple," her voice whispered in Jessie's mind. "Now, follow."

With a flick of her tail she began to swim through the clear blue water. Down, down, down.

Jessie swam after her. She swam more easily than she ever had in her own world. Her long red hair streamed behind her as she cut through the cool water like a fish. She had never felt so at home in the sea.

As they swam deeper, the light grew dimmer, until everything was blues and greens. Long strands of seaweed trailed across their path. Tiny fish circled them.

"Where are we going?" Jessie tried to call. But her voice was lost in the water. Ripple swam on.

Jessie tried again. But this time she remembered where she was. She didn't say the words aloud. This time she *thought* them, as hard as she could.

Ripple slowed, then drifted around to face her. "We are going to the crystal palaces," Jessie felt her say. "Is that not what you wish?"

"I . . ." Jessie didn't quite know how to answer. She didn't know exactly where she needed to go. All she knew was that she had to find a wish-stone as quickly as possible. Time was running out.

"Time . . . wish-stone?" said Ripple.

Jessie jumped. But then she realized that of course the mermaid could hear what she was thinking. She nodded. "I am here to find a wish-stone."

Ripple pressed her hands together. Jessie could feel her worry and sadness.

"The stones you seek come from far away, in the deep Under-Sea, outside the Bay," she said. "And for long and long, they have not come into our waters. The tides still bring them in from outside, but they do not reach us. They are all drawn in—to the Island."

Jessie felt a stab of terrible disappointment. "Oh no!" she exclaimed.

Ripple clutched her hands to her chest. Jessie's pain had hurt her as if it were her own.

"Ripple, what's the matter?"

A small gold-colored fish swam up to them and started nosing the mermaid anxiously. He had felt her distress too.

He looked crossly at Jessie. "What have you been doing to Ripple?" he thought at her, in a piping, bubbly voice.

Jessie shook her head. "Nothing!" she said. "I just felt—sad."

"Well, don't!" piped the fish. "Keep your human thoughts to yourself. Don't go round hurting others with them. *If* you don't mind."

He left Ripple and moved closer to Jessie. He was a very funny-looking fish, she thought. His golden body was small and round, and his tail and fins were very big and flappy. He had wide, poppy eyes and a bossy sort of expression.

"Don't be so rude!" he snapped. "You're not so good-looking yourself. Look at those legs. Two of them! And not a fin to be seen. Yuck!"

Oh dear, thought Jessie. I'll really have to learn not to think so loudly down here.

"Yes, you will," said the fish, as though she'd spoken aloud. Then he looked at her suspiciously. "And anyway, how did you find your way here? No human has been to Under-Sea for many long years."

Jessie lifted her chin. "My Realm friends brought me," she answered proudly. "I am Jessie, the granddaughter of Queen Jessica and Robert Belairs."

what to do?

The little fish's big eyes popped. "Seaweed and thunder!" he gasped. "Robert's grandchild!" He swam round and round her, staring.

"Did you know my grandfather?" Jessie asked.

"*Know* him? Of course I did," the fish said. "I was his guide times without number, in Under-Sea. I showed him things no other human has ever seen. The coral gardens. The crystal palaces. The Living Wall. Ah . . . we had great times together."

"We all loved Robert, in Under-Sea," said Ripple, gliding up to join them. "We were very sorry that he couldn't come back to see us any more."

67

"My fins we were," sighed the fish. He turned to Jessie. "And now his granddaughter is here," he said. "Come to see the sights. Well, I'll be glad to show them to you."

"Jessie hasn't come to see the sights," Ripple told him. "She's come to try to find a wish-stone."

The fish flicked his tail. "You know there's no chance of that," he said. "Lorca's grabbed every one that's come into the Bay for the last fifty years."

Jessie felt desperate. "Will you guide me to the Island, then?" she demanded. She knew she shouldn't even think of it. She knew what Patrice and Maybelle and Giff would say if they knew. But what else could she do?

"We cannot do that," Ripple's voice breathed in her mind. "We cannot go near the Island."

"But I need a wish-stone so *badly*," cried Jessie. "My home—Queen Jessica's home—is in danger. Only a wish-stone can help me save it!"

"Look, I think you should come with us to the crystal palaces," said the little fish. "We'll discuss the matter there."

He darted away in a flash of gold. Ripple

smiled at Jessie through her floating, billowing hair. "Follow," she sang, beckoning. "Follow."

Jessie followed.

Arriving at the place Ripple and the golden fish called "the crystal palaces" was exactly like walking into the Robert Belairs painting hanging in the hallway at Blue Moon.

There were the gardens of seaweed and coral, the fish flitting around like birds, the merpeople gliding through the blue water. And there were the palaces themselves, their crystal spires shining blue and silver.

Mermaids and mermen clustered around Jessie and Ripple, smiling and sending messages of greeting.

All of them had the same bright, unblinking blue eyes, but their hair was of many different colors — from light brown, like Ripple's, to black, dark brown, blue-gray, soft yellow, white and even pale green. Their tails were all different too. Some were silver, some were gold, some were spotted or striped with blue, green or purple.

The tiny-finned fairy creatures that Jessie had seen in her grandfather's Under-Sea painting were there too. They laughed and dived around her head, sometimes riding on their seahorses, sometimes leaping off and swinging on her floating hair.

"They love your hair," Ripple's voice laughed in Jessie's mind. "No one in Under-Sea has hair the color of the sunset."

Jessie was pleased. Her hair had never been described in such a lovely way before.

Ripple took her by the hand and led her a little away from the crowd to where two older merpeople were sitting together on a smooth rock.

As she came closer to them, Jessie realized that she had seen them before, sitting on that same rock. They were the merpeople her grandfather had painted playing with their child.

"Jessie, please greet Aqua and Storm, my mother and father," said Ripple, bowing her head.

Jessie jumped. Her mother and father? Then Ripple must have been the brown-haired child in the picture. Of course, many years had passed since it was painted. Ripple had grown up. She looked around for the other mermaid in the group, the one with shining black hair. Jessie knew that she would not look very different. In the Realm, people didn't age as they did in the mortal world.

"Mother and Father, please greet Jessie, granddaughter of Queen Jessica and Robert Belairs," Ripple was saying.

Warm feelings flowed to Jessie from Aqua and Storm as they smiled at her. They were strong and beautiful-looking. Aqua's silver hair was like a floating curtain that fell almost to the tip of her tail. Storm's hair was long too, but it was bound back with a string of plaited grass.

"We are pleased to greet you, Jessie." Aqua's rich voice said. "It is long and long since we saw a human here. And your grandfather was our dear friend. He often shared a meal with us."

"Mother and Father," Ripple said softly, "Jessie has come to us for help. Her home is in danger. She needs to find a wish-stone."

Aqua and Storm looked at one another, and Jessie caught some of the thoughts that passed between them. Wish-stone — Island — Lorca. Then a terrible, aching sadness. And a picture of a young mermaid with shining black hair.

Jessie looked at Ripple and felt a sadness in her too. She hesitated, confused and worried.

"They're thinking of their lost daughter."

Jessie spun around to see the little golden fish at her ear.

"Lost?" she whispered.

"Coral, Ripple's older sister, was lost long and long ago," he told her. "The first of many creatures lost to Under-Sea since the Island came."

"Lorca took Ripple's *sister*?" cried Jessie. She looked in horror at Aqua and Storm, and at Ripple. Their wide, unblinking blue eyes stared back at her, filled with pain.

She remembered Giff and Maybelle talking about a young mermaid who had disappeared. This must have been Coral.

"She is a prisoner on the Island," whispered Ripple. "Still, after all these years. Sometimes, at night, we hear her singing. Sad, sad and far away."

Jessie was filled with anger. "Why don't you try to get her back?" she cried.

"We tried, when we first realized what had happened." Aqua's voice was despairing. "We used every wish-stone left in Under-Sea to try to break Lorca's power. But it was no use."

"Then you should go to the Island yourselves," Jessie urged, "and *force* Lorca to give Coral up!"

They shook their heads. "We cannot breathe the air," they said together. "We cannot walk the land. Lorca is safe from us, on her Island."

"Then ask Queen Helena to help you!" Jessie exclaimed. "She could send her guards, in a boat. They could . . ."

But again they were shaking their heads. "The sea and the land are separate in the Realm," they said together. "The Folk cannot help us. That is the Rule."

Jessie frowned crossly. She was starting to get very impatient with the Rule.

"Lorca has captured many creatures," Storm said. "But Coral was the first. And the only mermaid to be taken. Now we are too careful to fall into Lorca's net. We keep away from the Island."

"The fish aren't too careful, though," the golden fish's piping, bubbling voice chimed in. "The young ones are easy prey for Lorca. Sometimes they escape her nets to tell the tale. That's how we know her name and what she does. But often they don't escape. And then they are lost."

"Coral was young and foolish too," sighed Aqua. "But so filled with life. Oh, how she loved to listen to Robert's stories of the mortal world, Storm. Seeing his granddaughter makes me remember."

Again a feeling of sadness swept over the little group.

"We are sorry," Storm said, putting his arm around Aqua's shoulders. "We would give you anything we had for Robert's sake, Jessie. But sadly a wish-stone is not in our power to grant."

"Once they were everywhere in Under-Sea," said Aqua. "Our Coral had them by the ten and twelve."

"I remember," Ripple put in. "I was only little, but I remember Coral's wish-stones. She carried them with her always, in a net made of her own hair. They were her treasures."

"Coral loved the wishing," said Aqua. "She loved new things. Different things. It hurts me to remember that we argued about it, the last time we saw each other. She said she was bored, stuck here in this quiet Bay. I was angry with her. It was the time of the blue moon. There was much to do."

Jessie looked up. Just like Mum and me this morning, she thought. How strange. I guess children and parents are the same, wherever they live.

"She swam away from me, angrily, toward the deep ocean," Aqua went on sadly. "I did not worry at first. I thought she would come back safely, as she had before. But I had not counted on Lorca. That very day the Island rose from the seabed. And I never saw Coral again." She put her face in her hands.

Storm touched her shoulder and bowed his head.

Jessie felt Ripple speaking to her. "Come away, Jessie. We need to talk."

"Ripple? I heard that! What are you planning?" piped the little golden fish, swimming after them as they glided away.

Ripple lifted her small, pointed chin and looked at him. There was a determined expression in her strange blue eyes. "Come with us and see," she said. "You might even be able to help. After all, you must have some uses, magic fish."

CHAPTER EIGHT

The Dark Shadow

"What did you call him?" Jessie tugged at Ripple's hand, making her stop and listen. "Magic fish? Why did you call him that?"

The little fish waggled his big tail importantly. "Because that's what I am!" he said.

"But—but Granny said you were really powerful," Jessie stammered. "And I was imagining you'd be . . . well, you know—bigger."

"Well!" huffed the fish. "Good things come in small packages, you know."

Suddenly, like a bolt of lightning, Jessie realized what all this meant. She didn't need to find a wish-stone any more. She'd found something much, much better.

"Oh," she screamed. "Then if you're the magic fish, you can grant my wish, can't you? You can save Blue Moon!"

The fish blew bubbles and shook his head. "Sadly, I'm no use to you," he said. "As I am no use to Aqua and Storm. Don't you think they would have used me to get Coral back, if they could? I can only grant wishes to people who catch me by accident, and then let me go again. That's the Rule."

The Rule again!

"That's crazy," Jessie shouted. "Crazy!"

The fish waved his fins. "I can't help that," he said. "It's always been the Rule. I'm surprised Queen Jessica didn't tell you about it."

Jessie stared at him. "Actually, she did," she admitted. "Or she tried to."

"*No use . . .*" Granny had called, trying to make her voice heard over the rushing of the Door. "*Magic fish . . . rules . . .*" She'd been trying to tell Jessie that the magic fish couldn't help her, because of the Rule.

"Why can you only grant wishes when you're caught by *accident*?" Jessie asked in despair.

"Think about it," said the fish scornfully. "How could I live otherwise? Everyone wants a wish now and then. If they could get three of them just by catching me whenever they felt like it, I'd never be out of a net! My life would be a misery."

"Yes, I can see that," whispered Jessie. She felt close to tears. Oh, I just don't know what to do, she thought. Soon I'll have to go home again. And I'm still no closer to finding a wish than I've ever been.

"Listen," said Ripple. "I've been thinking. I think you should try to get onto the Island."

"Well, I think so too!" exclaimed Jessie. "But I'll never find the way on my own. And you said—"

"That was before," Ripple said grimly.

"Before what?" Jessie asked.

"Before I realized something—just now, when we were talking to my mother and father. The Rule forbids us from asking Realm Folk to help in our domain. But you're *not* of the Realm, Jessie. You're human." She paused.

"Oh no," mumbled the magic fish. "Ripple, no!"

But Ripple ignored him. "So I'll lead you to the Island, Jessie, on one condition. When we get there, you can find your wish-stone. But then — you have to help me get Coral back!"

"You're crazy, Ripple!" The magic fish was so upset that he started swimming in circles. "You can't risk going to the Island. And you can't let Jessie risk it either."

Jessie and Ripple faced him and linked arms.

"We're going," Ripple said. "And that's that."

Jessie nodded.

"I'll tell your mother and father," warned the fish.

"No you will not," snapped Ripple. "Or I'll never speak to you again! Don't you realize that Jessie is our only chance to save Coral, magic fish?"

She stared at him with fierce blue eyes.

He waved his fins helplessly.

"Don't you want Coral home with us again?" Ripple went on. "Don't you want my mother and father to be happy?"

"Of course I do," the little fish said. He sighed and blew a bubble. "All right. I'll help you. But I don't like it. I don't like it at all."

Jessie didn't have any idea where she was. She just swam after Ripple and the magic fish wherever they led. They brushed their way through trailing seaweed branches, following some sort of trail that only they could see.

The water was rougher now. It was also sandy and full of tiny bubbles. It was hard to see very far ahead. So it was a shock to Jessie when suddenly she felt Ripple's fear.

"What is it, what is it?" she called, swimming forward as fast as she could.

"The Island is very close," Ripple's voice sighed in her head. "See . . . there . . ."

Jessie squinted through the cloudy water and saw a dark shadow rising up in front of them.

"What will we do now?" she asked.

"Swim away as fast as we can, if you ask me," grumbled the magic fish.

"No!" sang Ripple. "Jessie, you must go to the surface. Climb up the rocks onto the Island. Try to find out where Coral is being kept prisoner. Then come back and tell us, so we can make a plan."

"I don't need to come back," Jessie objected. "We can talk with our minds."

"No we can't. This way of talking does not work between land and sea," Ripple told her. "Once you are on land we will not be able to hear your thoughts, and you will not be able to hear ours."

They had stopped swimming, but they were still moving closer and closer to the dark shadow ahead. And they were moving fast.

"The tide is strong," warned the magic fish, beating his fins against the current. "It's pulling us in to the Island, Ripple. Much too quickly. We had better—"

His words broke off with a shout of fear.

Jessie's head echoed with the shock of it, and with Ripple's terror and her own. Because suddenly they were tumbling toward each other, crashing together, knocking heads and bodies helplessly.

Jessie felt Ripple's tail lashing against her legs. She felt the magic fish, hopelessly tangled in her streaming red hair, struggling to free himself.

Then they were being dragged along—not just by the current, but by something else, something they could feel but couldn't see.

"A net!" Ripple cried. "We're caught in a net!"

"Help me!" bubbled the magic fish. "Help me!"

With all her strength, Jessie tore against the web that had trapped them. But it was terribly strong. As it pushed against her face, she saw it— a fine black net that was almost invisible in the dark, cloudy water.

Panic swept over her. She started beating against the net, thinking of nothing except escape, feeling the others struggling in the same way, knowing it was hopeless.

And then, crystal clear in her mind, came the

memory of her mother's voice; familiar, ordinary, full of human common sense. *"Panic is the real killer,"* Rosemary had said in the kitchen this morning. *"When people panic, they forget to think."*

Even in a magic world, that was true. Jessie knew she had to think. Stop struggling helplessly. Stop screaming and crying for help that couldn't come. Think!

She grabbed the panic-stricken Ripple with one hand. She put her arm around her and held her close. At least that way they wouldn't crash against one another. "Be still," she thought. "Be still!"

As she felt Ripple quieten she put her other hand behind her head and pulled at her hair, untangling it so the magic fish could swim free. His bubbling cries stopped as her fingers did their work. He darted, gasping, over her shoulder and took shelter between her and Ripple.

Then, clinging together, they let the net pull them in.

The dark shadow grew closer and closer.

"We're going to crash into the rocks!" thought

Jessie, and panic nearly seized her again. But then she saw that there was a patch in the shadow that was even darker than the rest.

It was a cave. And they were being dragged toward it!

"The Island is hollow," Jessie told the others. "We're being pulled inside it. Hold on!"

Then with a rush they were plunging into blackness. They heard the whisper of something closing behind them, sealing the cave, trapping them inside.

Ripple screamed. Jessie shut her eyes tightly. The magic fish shuddered against her chest.

And then they were spinning and going up. Above them, someone was hauling them in.

The spinning rush upward stopped. The net that held Jessie, Ripple and the magic fish hung swinging in the water.

Jessie opened her eyes. She was dizzy and weak. Just above her, she could see the surface. And there was light, but it wasn't sunlight.

Without warning, the net that held her tangled with Ripple and the magic fish dropped away. Jessie didn't realize what had happened at first.

Then she understood.

They no longer needed to be held in the net because they were in an underground lake. The cave that was the entrance to the lake had been sealed with a door of some kind. Now they were trapped—inside the Island.

Other creatures were in the lake too. Although she couldn't see them, Jessie could feel their thoughts. Maybe they were hiding—or maybe they were being held in some other part of the lake.

"Coral! Coral! Are you here?" Ripple had felt the other creatures too. She was calling her sister.

But there was no answer.

"She isn't here," said the magic fish. "Lorca must be keeping her in some other place."

"How do we know she's on the Island at all?" asked Jessie.

"We know," said the fish grimly. "That net—the net that caught us—was made of her hair."

Jessie felt sick.

Ripple clung to her, shivering with fear. Jessie put her arm around her shoulders. What was going to happen now?

"Come to me!" thundered a voice from above them. "Come to me!"

escape

Holding Ripple and the magic fish, Jessie let herself drift slowly upward. She knew there was no point in hiding. There was no way out of this trap.

Her head broke through the surface of the lake. She looked around. They were in the center of a huge cave. Darkness gloomed at its sides and in its rocky ceiling, but around the lake hundreds of candles burned. Their flickering light lit up the water's surface and played on the speckled gray wish-stones that lay heaped around the lake's shore.

But Jessie barely glanced at the wish-stones. All her attention was fixed on the figure that stared down at them from a rocky platform. A woman with flowing hair and gown, her face in deep shadow. She was leaning forward, searching the water to see what she had caught.

"I am Lorca, little fish!" cried the woman. "Welcome!" Her voice echoed from the rocky walls of the cave.

"We are not fish," called Jessie. "Lorca! Let us go!"

The woman jumped back as if someone had hit her.

"What?" she cried. "Mermaids? Oh no! No! What have I done?" She fell to her knees and buried her face in her hands.

Jessie and Ripple looked at one another. This was not what they had expected.

The magic fish wriggled out of Jessie's grasp and stuck its golden head out of the water.

"Let us go, Lorca!" he piped angrily, thrashing his tail. "Let us go, and all the other creatures you have taken."

Lorca's head jerked up. She gasped. "Can this be true?" her booming voice echoed. "Have I caught you, magic fish? At last?"

"What do you mean, at last?" bubbled the magic fish.

"I have been casting my nets for you, all these long years." The voice was like the beating of a drum. "I have waited so long. Now I have you! At last! I have you—and I will set you free. And so I claim my wishes."

"If you have been fishing for me, you cannot claim your wishes," bubbled the magic fish. "By the Rule, I must be caught by accident."

"No!" Lorca's shout was deafening. "No! This is the only way! The only way! I have tried the wish-stones. I have gathered a hundred of them, but they do nothing. Nothing!"

Jessie pulled at the magic fish's tail and made him put his head below the surface again so that they could speak in secret.

"For goodness' sake, fish, don't tell her you can't

grant the wishes," she told him fiercely. "If she thinks she can have what she wants, she'll let us go!"

"We cannot go without Coral," Ripple insisted. "If we get away, we must take her with us. You must ask for that, magic fish. You must . . ."

"I cannot lie," said the fish. "It is the Rule."

"Fish, our lives are at stake! Forget the Rule for once," Jessie exploded. "And anyway, even if Lorca *has* been fishing for you for years, she didn't know when or if she'd catch you, did she? So this *was* an accident, in a way. How do you know the magic won't work for her?"

"What if it does? It may be worse than if it does not," murmured Ripple, her thoughts filled with fear. "Because what will Lorca wish for? Something so great that even a hundred wish-stones cannot do it. It could be something of great evil."

"She could wish to spread her power over the whole of Under-Sea," suggested the fish with a shudder.

"Why would she want to do that?" asked

Jessie. "What use could she make of the power? She's a land person, like me. She breathes air and has no fins or tail. She can't . . ." She broke off. She put her head above the surface again and looked at Lorca. A wild idea had come into her mind.

Her thoughts began to race, tumbling over each other. Yes. Yes, it could be . . .

But what if she was wrong? She was tired, and weak from the struggles in the net. Did she dare to risk facing that frightening figure on the rocky platform? Letting her know that she was not a mermaid at all, but human?

Well, she had to try. All their lives depended on it. And so did Blue Moon. Even now Granny must be wondering where she was. Even now the fire must be getting closer, closer . . . She began swimming quietly to the edge of the lake.

"What are you going to do?" Ripple called after her in terror. "Are you still trying to get a wishstone? Jessie, don't get out of the water! She cannot get to you in here. Out there, she can—"

"Don't worry, Ripple," Jessie called back. "Just wait. If I'm right . . ."

Slowly she pulled herself onto the rocky shore.

Her legs trembled as she climbed toward the shadowy figure standing above her. She had been a long time under the sea, and she had grown used to swimming instead of walking.

A shriek echoed from the rocky platform.

"A human! But . . . ?"

Jessie shivered with cold and fear. She forced her shaking legs to take the last few steps. The woman in the shadows drew breath sharply as she came closer.

"Stay back, human child," cried Lorca. "Are you not afraid? Do you not know who I am?"

Jessie looked her full in the face. She was beautiful. Her long black hair fell like a curtain around her slim shoulders. Her white feet were small and bare. Her blue eyes were filled with terrible sorrow.

"Yes, I do," Jessie answered. She heard her own voice echoing against the rocks. It sounded deep and strange. "I know who you are and I know what you've done," she said, staring straight into the sad blue eyes. "Once, long ago, you took wish-stones and wished. You wished for what you have now. And then you found you didn't want it after all. But the wish couldn't be undone."

The figure before her groaned.

"I know who you are and I know what your name is," Jessie went on softly. "Now you call yourself Lorca. But years ago, in Under-Sea, your name was Coral."

There was a scream from the lake. It was Ripple. She had heard everything. "Coral," she was sobbing. "Coral! Sister!"

"Ripple," breathed Lorca. She began to clamber down the rocks, scratching and bruising her feet and legs. She threw herself down by the edge of the lake, reaching out.

Ripple held up her arms. Lorca went toward her. Her hair fell over her shoulders like a heavy black veil. "Ripple, my little sister. I did not know you. I did not know . . ."

"My grandfather, Robert Belairs, told you stories about the human world, didn't he?" Jessie said.

"Yes," whispered Lorca. "I thought he could take me there. My mother and I had an argument. I ran away. I was so angry." She gave a shuddering sigh. "I took all my wish-stones and made my wishes," she said. "I wished I could breathe air and walk on land. I wished for an island near the mouth of the Bay, where I could wait for Robert. I didn't think. I didn't remember the wish-stone Rule. I had never wished for anything important before."

The magic fish made a sad, bubbling sound.

"I wished for a new name," Lorca went on. "A name made of the same letters as my own, but different, and not like the names of Under-Sea. And my wishes were granted. So Lorca of the Island was born."

"But Robert never came to the Island," said Jessie, "because he left the Realm with Princess Jessica that very day. And he couldn't come back."

Lorca bowed her head. "And then—oh, then I began to miss the sea," she cried. "I missed the soft water. I missed my family, my friends. I wanted to be able to swim again, and see the coral and the palaces, and feel the voices of the people I loved."

She drew a deep breath. "I did not like the land. The bright sun hurt my eyes. I hid away from it down here, in this cave. I tried to wish myself back to Under-Sea. I tried with one wish-stone, with ten, with a hundred. But . . ." Her voice trailed away.

"That's why you've been trying to catch the magic fish," sighed Ripple. "Because only he is powerful enough to undo the wish-stone magic."

"Of course!" cried Lorca. "He was my last hope. I wove nets from my hair and threw them into the sea. Those fish I caught I kept, for company. I was so lonely! But the one I really wanted, the magic fish, I never caught. Until this day."

She tore at her long black hair. "And now he says he cannot help me. So I must stay as Lorca forever. And I can never go home again."

Jessie felt her eyes filling with tears.

The magic fish was swimming in small circles of distress. "Coral — Lorca," he bubbled. "I am sorry. But the Rule . . ."

"You don't know for sure!" exclaimed Jessie. "The magic might still work. Try, Lorca. Just try!"

Lorca stared at her, her beautiful face filled with half-fearful hope. She clasped her hands together. She closed her eyes.

"I wish . . ." she began, and swallowed. "I wish — that I — that Lorca of the Island may become Coral of Under-Sea once more."

They waited, holding their breath. The seconds ticked by.

It's not going to happen, thought Jessie. Oh, I can't bear it! She spun round to the magic fish. "You *must* be able to help," she raged. "Forget about the Rule just for once."

The fish looked at her helplessly.

"You were caught and freed," Jessie begged. "Isn't that enough? Oh magic fish, *please* make Lorca's wish come true!"

The fish leaped in the water. "Caught and freed! Yes! Jessie!" he bubbled. "Jessie . . . !"

But before he could say any more there was a low, rumbling, growling sound. Pieces of rock began falling from the ceiling of the cave and splashing into the lake.

"What's happening?" Jessie screamed. "What's gone wrong?"

"The Island! It's sinking!" squeaked the fish.

The rumbling grew louder. The ground on which Jessie and Lorca were standing began to tremble. With a crack the rock split under their feet.

"Dive!" shrieked Ripple.

Jessie snatched Lorca's hand and jumped into the lake. Then they were all swimming for their lives, surrounded by hundreds of other fish that had come streaming in from the sides of the lake.

They raced for the cave that was the entrance to the open sea. Down, down, they swam, as rocks plunged into the lake after them. They darted through the torn net gate, out of the cave entrance.

And then, with seconds to spare, they were plunging into safe water, as Lorca's Island tumbled to the ocean bed behind them.

Jessie spun around to look. Where once the dark shadow had been there was now only cloudy, bubbling water and a pile of rocks and sand. Below the rocks, she knew, the wish-stones lay buried. No one could find them now.

And only then did she remember.

Lorca! she thought, in confusion. Lorca has no coral necklace. She won't be able to breathe. She'll drown.

"No she won't, Jessie!"

"No I won't, Jessie!"

The sweet voices sang in her mind. Soft white hands touched hers. She looked around. She saw Ripple's smile, her floating light brown hair, a flashing silver tail. And beside her, another smile, a cloud of shining black hair, sparkling blue eyes — and another silver tail.

She blinked.

Lorca was gone. Coral was a mermaid again.

A flash of gold beside her caught her eye. It was the magic fish.

"So," she said. "You decided the Rule could be bent after all."

"No," his bubbling voice piped in her ear. "No, Jessie, you don't understand. You—"

"Home!" sang Ripple and Coral, diving and plunging in the blue-green water. "We're going home!"

Home, thought Jessie. Blue Moon. Granny. Mum. *Home*. Her heart ached. She hadn't found what she'd come for in Under-Sea, but suddenly she wanted to be home more than anything in the world. The danger must be very close, now. She was needed there, she had to go. But home seemed so far away.

I wish I was home, right now, she thought, I so wish . . .

The water swirled in front of her eyes. She couldn't see. What's happening? she thought in panic.

"Jessie! Jessie! Where are you? Where . . . ?"

She could hear the mermaids' voices calling, but faintly.

"Goodbye, Jessie," bubbled the magic fish. "I'll tell the others — Ripple, Coral, your friends waiting on the shore. I'll tell them . . . about the wishes . . . your hair . . . goodbye . . . goodbye . . . thank you. . ."

And then his voice too had died away.

CHAPTER TEN

The Third Wish

Jessie opened her eyes. She blinked in the bright, bright sunlight. She was sitting on the grass in the secret garden. The air smelled of burning leaves and rosemary. Fire-engine sirens howled in the distance.

"Jessie!" Granny was bending over her, stroking her dripping hair. "Oh, Jessie, I've been so worried about you. I should never have let you go. Jessie, we've got to leave here. The fires are coming."

Jessie shook her head, trying to clear it. Drops of salt water sprayed the dry grass. She touched her neck. The coral necklace was gone. "How did

I get here?" she murmured. "How . . . ?"

"Don't worry about that now," begged Granny. "Just come."

Jessie stumbled after her as she hurried out of the secret garden, up through the tall trees toward the house. Her mind was racing.

Somehow the magic fish had sent her home. But how? He'd said he couldn't grant wishes just because people asked for them.

But then a few of the things he'd said hadn't been true. He'd said Lorca couldn't make a wish, because she hadn't caught him by accident. And yet her wish to turn back into Coral had been granted.

How strange. He'd been so certain. And it was true that, at first, Jessie had thought he was right. On the Island Lorca had made her wish, but nothing had happened for ages. In fact, nothing had happened till . . .

Jessie stopped. Her jaw dropped. Could it be . . . ?

"Come *on*, Jessie!" shouted Granny from the house.

What had the magic fish called to her as she disappeared from Under-Sea? *"I'll tell them,"* he'd bubbled. *"I'll tell them . . . about the wishes . . . your hair . . ."*

Jessie thought it through. When they had first been caught in Lorca's net, the magic fish had got tangled in her hair. He had been struggling and panicking.

She had been panicking too. But then she'd remembered her mother's words and calmed down. She had soothed Ripple, then she had quietly freed the fish from her hair.

She had *caught* him accidentally. And then she had *freed* him.

She, not Lorca, had been given the three wishes.

Please make Lorca's wish come true! she had cried to the magic fish. That was the first wish, and it had been granted.

I wish I was home, right now she had thought. That was the second wish. And it had been granted too.

Jessie took a breath. She could see Granny running back from the house toward her, calling. The sun beat down overhead. The hot wind blew in her face, bringing with it the smell of smoke.

It was time for the third wish.

"I wish it would rain!" Jessie yelled with all her might. "I wish it would rain and rain until the fires are out!"

There was a shimmer in the air. The whole earth seemed to be holding its breath. And then, where blue sky had been, there was only gray. And the rain was falling. Slowly at first, and then faster and faster. Heavy, steady, cool rain.

Jessie stood in it, hugging Granny, laughing with happiness as the water soaked them both. They watched the rain washing the dry leaves, cooling the hot grass. And they imagined that same rain splashing on hungry flames all over the Mountains, so that they hissed, and grew small, and finally died.

"You found a wish-stone!" Granny breathed.

"No, I didn't," said Jessie.

Granny turned to her in amazement. "Then how —" she began.

"Jessie! Mum!" called a voice. They looked back toward the house. Rosemary was standing there, laughing at them.

"What are you two *doing*?" she shouted.

Jessie grinned. "Getting wet! Again!" she called. She ran through the tall trees, up the steps that led to Blue Moon, and into her mother's arms.

Rosemary hugged her tightly. She didn't seem to care that Jessie was dripping wet.

"Oh, Jessie, the rain!" she sighed. "Oh, isn't it wonderful? And it was so sudden. Like magic."

Jessie snuggled against her. "Magic is useful," she said. "But human common sense helps a lot too."

Rosemary stroked her daughter's tangled, wet hair. That was a strange thing to say, she thought. But she decided not to ask any questions. It had been a long, hot day, and Jessie was probably over-tired. It was a shame she hadn't been able to have a swim.

Two days later, Jessie woke to find that the rain had stopped in the night. The morning sun was beaming through her window. The curtains fluttered in a light breeze. Everything outside looked fresh and new.

She saw something lying on her desk. She got out of bed and went to look. It was the sundress she had left on the shore of the Bay. It was clean, ironed and folded, and smelled of flowers.

"Thank you, Patrice," she whispered. She picked up the dress and took it to her cupboard. As she hung it up she felt something in the pocket—something small and hard, wrapped in a scrap of silk.

She pulled it out and unwrapped it. It was a tiny golden fish. Another charm for her bracelet. Another gift from the Realm, so she'd never forget.

Jessie held the little fish to her cheek for a moment. The memories of Under-Sea came flooding back.

She shivered as she remembered Lorca's Island. She smiled as she thought of Ripple and Coral, Aqua and Storm, the crystal palaces, the coral gardens, the tiny water-fairies on their seahorses, the ride down the river. She laughed aloud at the memory of the magic fish.

"You sound happy," said her mother at the door.

Jessie turned around. "I am," she said. "I'm so, so happy."

"It's going to be a lovely day," Rosemary went on. "And I'm not working this morning. Would you like to go to the pool? It's been ages since you had a swim."

Jessie laughed again. "I'd *love* a swim," she said. "In fact, I can't think of anything I'd rather do."

"You see? Wishes *can* come true," teased Rosemary.

Jessie looked at the little golden fish in her hand and at the other charms on her bracelet.

"Yes," she said. "I know."

Turn the page for a peek at
Jessie's next adventure in the

Fairy Realm:

BOOK 4

The Last
fairy-apple Tree

"The fairy-apple trees," murmured Jessie's grandmother. The charm bracelet on her wrist jingled softly as she lifted her hand to touch the painting on the wall in front of her.

She glanced at Jessie's curious face and smiled, her green eyes twinkling as they always did when she spoke about magic things.

"I haven't told you about that part of the Realm, have I, Jessie?", she said. "About Hidden Valley, and the gnomes, and the fairy-apple trees?"

Jessie stood in the pool of morning sunlight that streamed through the window of the spare bedroom at Blue Moon and watched her grandmother's slim fingers trace the outlines of the trees in the painting.

"Fairy-apple trees!" she exclaimed. "Are they where fairy-apple jelly comes from?"

Her mouth watered as she thought about fairy-apple jelly. It was one of her favorite things in all the world: a clear, sweet, golden-pink jelly you spread on fresh bread.

Granny had made fairy-apple jelly for as long as Jessie could remember. She made it from fruit she gathered from a neighbor's tree. And in winter, small, glistening jars of it were always lined up on a shelf in the Blue Moon pantry.

Jessie's mother, Rosemary, always said that "fairy-apple" was just Granny's name for ordinary apple jelly. But Jessie could see that the apples on the trees in the painting weren't ordinary. They were very small and round, and a beautiful gold-red color.

"I didn't know fairy-apples grew in the Realm too," she said.

Granny smiled dreamily. "Oh, that's where all the fairy-apple trees grow," she said. "All but one."

EMILY RODDA

has written many books for children, including the Rowan of Rin books. She has won the Children's Book Council of Australia Book of the Year Award an unprecedented five times. A former editor, Ms. Rodda is also the best-selling author of adult mysteries under the name Jennifer Rowe. She lives in Australia.

LOWER MILLS